BEDTIME STORIES

BEDTIME STORIES

Terry Jones

Nanette Newman

illustrated by

Michael Foreman

PAVILION CHILDREN'S BOOKS

This edition published in Great Britain in 2002 by
Pavilion Children's Books
A member of Chrysalis Books plc
64 Brewery Road
London N7 9NT
www.pavilionbooks.co.uk

Designed by Bet Ayer
Assistant Designer Imogen Chester
Cover design by Sarah Goodwin

A CIP catalogue record for this book is available
from the British Library.

ISBN 1 86205 276 X

Set in Garamond
Printed in Hong Kong by C&C Offset

2 4 6 8 10 9 7 5 3

This book can be ordered direct from the publisher. Please contact
the Marketing Department. But try your bookshop first.

Contents

The
Sea Tiger

Terry Jones

here was once a tiger who told the most enormous lies. No matter how hard he tried, he just couldn't tell the truth.

Once the monkey asked the tiger where he was going. The tiger replied that he was on his way to the moon, where he kept a store of tiger-cheese which made his eyes brighter than the sun so that he could see in the dark. But in fact he was going behind a bush for a snooze.

Another time, the snake asked the tiger round for lunch, but the tiger said that he couldn't come because a man had heard him singing in the jungle, and had asked him to go to the big city that very afternoon to sing in the opera.

'Oh!' said the snake. 'Before you go, won't you sing something for me?'

'Ah no,' said the tiger. 'If I sing before I've had my breakfast, my tail swells up and turns into a sausage, and I get followed around by sausage-flies all day.'

One day, all the animals in the jungle held a meeting, and decided they'd cure the tiger of telling such enormous lies. So they sent the monkey off to find the wizard who lived in the snow-capped mountains.

The monkey climbed for seven days and seven nights, and he got higher and higher until at last he reached the cave in the snow where the wizard lived.

At the entrance to the cave he called out: 'Old wizard, are you there?'

And a voice called out: 'Come in, monkey, I've been expecting you.'

So the monkey went into the cave. He found the wizard busy
preparing spells, and he told him that the animals of the jungle
wanted to cure the tiger of telling such enormous lies.

'Very well,' said the wizard. 'Take this potion and pour it into
the tiger's ears when he is asleep.'

'But what will it do, wizard?' asked the monkey.
The wizard smiled and said: 'Rest assured, once you've given
him this potion, everything the tiger says will be true all right.'

So the monkey took the potion and went back to the jungle, where he told the other animals what they had to do.

That day, while the tiger was having his usual nap behind the bush, all the other animals gathered round in a circle, and the monkey crept up very cautiously to the tiger and carefully poured a little of the potion first into one of the tiger's ears and then into the other. Then he ran back to the other animals, and they all called out: 'Tiger! Tiger! Wake up, tiger!'

After a while, the tiger opened one eye, and then the other. He was a bit surprised to find all the other animals of the jungle standing around him in a circle.

'Have you been asleep?' asked the lion.

'Oh no,' said the tiger, 'I was just lying here, planning my next expedition to the bottom of the ocean.'

When they heard this, all the other animals shook their heads and said: 'The wizard's potion hasn't worked. Tiger's still telling as whopping lies as ever!'

But just then the tiger found himself leaping to his feet and bounding across the jungle. 'But it's true!' he cried to his own surprise.

'What are you doing, tiger?' they asked.

'I'm going to fly there!' he called and, sure enough, he spread out his legs and soared up high above the trees and across the top of the jungle.

Now if there's one thing tigers don't like, it's heights, and so the tiger yelled out: 'Help! I am flying! Get me down!'

But he found himself flying on and on until the jungle was far behind him and he flew over the snow-capped mountains where the wizard lived. The wizard looked up at the tiger flying overhead and smiled to himself and said: 'Ha-ha, old tiger, you'll always tell the truth now. For anything you say will become true – even if it wasn't before!'

And the tiger flew on and on, and he got colder and colder, and if there's one thing tigers hate worse than heights, it's being cold.

At length he found himself flying out over the sea, and then suddenly he dropped like a stone until he came down splash in the middle of the ocean. Now if there's one thing that tigers hate more than heights and cold, it's getting wet.

'Urrrrgh!' said the tiger, but down and down he sank, right to the bottom of the ocean, and all the fish came up to him and stared, so he chased them off with his tail.

Then he looked up and he could see the bottom of the waves high above him, and he swam up and up, and just as he was running out of breath, he reached the surface. Then he struggled and splashed and tried to swim for the shore.

Just then a fishing boat came by, and all the fishermen gasped in amazement to see a tiger swimming in the middle of the ocean. Then one of them laughed and pointed at the tiger and said: 'Look! A sea tiger!'

And they all laughed and pointed at the tiger, and if there's one thing tigers hate worse than heights and cold and getting wet, it's being laughed at.

The poor tiger paddled away as fast as he could, but it was a long way to the shore, and eventually the fishermen threw one of their nets over him, and hauled him on to the boat.

'Oh ho!' they laughed. 'Now we can make a fortune by getting this sea tiger to perform tricks in the circus!'

Now this made the tiger really angry, because if there's one thing tigers hate more than heights and cold and getting wet and being laughed at, it's performing tricks in the circus.

So as soon as they landed, he tore up the net, and leapt out
of the boat, and ran home to the forest as fast as his legs would
carry him.

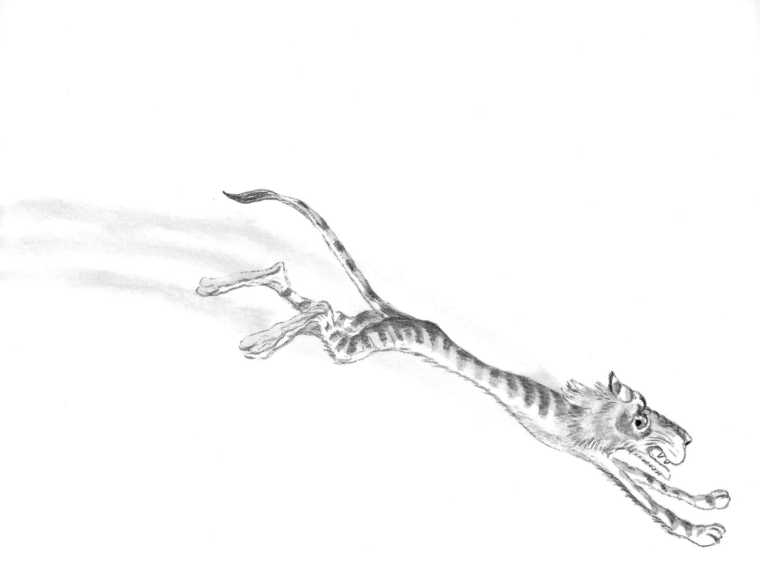

And he never told any lies, *ever* again.

A Fish
of the World

Terry Jones

 herring once decided to swim right round the world. 'I'm tired of the North Sea,' he said. 'I want to find out what else there is in the world.'

So he swam off south into the deep Atlantic. He swam and he swam, far far away from the seas he knew, through the warm waters of the Equator and on down into the South Atlantic. And all the time he saw many strange and wonderful fish that he had never seen before. Once he was nearly eaten by a shark, and once he was nearly electrocuted by an electric eel, and once he was nearly stung by a sting-ray.

But he swam on and on, round the tip of Africa and into the
Indian Ocean.
And he passed by devilfish and sailfish and sawfish and

38

swordfish and bluefish and blackfish and mudfish and
sunfish, and he was amazed by the different shapes
and sizes and colours.

On he swam, into the Java Sea, and he saw fish that leapt out of the water and fish that lived at the bottom of the sea and fish that could walk on their fins.

And on he swam, through the Coral Sea, where the shells of millions and millions of tiny creatures had turned to rock and stood as big as mountains.

But still he swam on, into the wide Pacific. He swam over the deepest parts of the ocean, where the water is so deep that it is inky black at the bottom, and the fish carry lanterns over their heads, and some have lights on their tails.

And through the Pacific he swam, and then he turned north
and headed up to the cold Siberian Sea, where huge white
icebergs sailed past him like mighty ships. And still he swam on
and on and into the frozen Arctic Ocean, where the sea is
forever covered in ice.

And on he went, past Greenland and Iceland, and finally he swam home into his own North Sea. All his friends and relations gathered round and made a great fuss of him. They had a big feast and offered him the very best food they could find.

But the herring just yawned and said: 'I've swum round the entire world. I have seen everything there is to see, and I have eaten more exotic and wonderful dishes than you could possibly imagine.' And he refused to eat anything.

47

Then his friends and relations begged him to come home and live with them, but he refused. 'I've been everywhere there is, and that old rock is too dull and small for me.' And he went off and lived on his own.

And when the breeding season came, he refused to join in the spawning, saying: 'I've swum round the entire world, and now I know how many fish there are in the world, I can't be interested in herrings any more.'

Eventually, one of the oldest of the herrings swam up to him, and said: 'Listen. If you don't spawn with us, some herrings' eggs will go unfertilized and will not turn into healthy young herring. If you don't live with your family, you'll make them sad. And if you don't eat, you'll die.'

But the herring said: 'I don't mind. I've been everywhere there is to go, I've seen everything there is to see, and now I know everything there is to know.'

The old fish shook his head. 'No one has ever seen everything there is to see,' he said, 'nor known everything there is to know.'

'Look,' said the herring, 'I've swum through the North Sea, the Atlantic Ocean, the Indian Ocean, the Java Sea, the Coral Sea, the great Pacific Ocean, the Siberian Sea and the frozen Arctic. Tell me, what else is there for me to see or know?'

'I don't know,' said the old herring, 'but there may be something.'

Well, just then a fishing boat came by, and the herrings

were caught in a net and taken to market that very day.

And a man bought the herring, and ate it for his supper.

And he never knew that it had swum right round the world, and had seen everything there was to see, and knew everything there was to know.

There's a Bear
in the Bath

Nanette Newman

Liza looked out of the window and saw a bear sitting in the garden, so she went outside and said, 'What are you doing in my garden?'

'I'm here for a visit,' said the bear.

'Why?' asked Liza.

'Why not?' asked the bear.

'I don't know,' said Liza.

'Exactly,' said the bear, 'and by the way – when bears come to visit they usually get invited in.'

'Oh, come in,' said Liza.

The bear looked round the kitchen.

'Would you like something to eat?' asked Liza.

'Like what?' asked the bear.

'Porridge,' said Liza.

'What makes you think that bears like porridge?'

'Well,' said Liza, 'when Goldilocks went to the three bears' house…'

'Oh, that,' said the bear. 'You didn't believe any of that, did you? You'll be saying next that all bears like honey.' He poured himself a cup of coffee.

'What's your name?' asked Liza.

'Jam,' said the bear.

'Nobody is called Jam,' said Liza.

'I am,' said the bear.

'How come?' asked Liza.

'My mother,' said the bear, helping himself to a chocolate biscuit, 'loved jam more than anything in the world – then she had me and she loved me more than anything in the world, so she called me Jam.'

'I see,' said Liza – not seeing at all – 'it just seems a funny name for a bear.'

But the bear wasn't listening – he'd turned on the radio and was dancing and spilling crisps everywhere.

He danced into the hall, twisting and twirling, and into the
living room, and then lay down on the sofa.

'You're a good dancer,' said Liza.

'I know,' said the bear. He picked up the newspaper.

'I'm brilliant at crosswords,' he said.

'That's showing off,' said Liza.

'What is?' asked the bear.

'Boasting about how good you are at something,' said Liza.

'Oh, no,' said the bear, 'boasting is very unattractive in a child – boasting when you're a bear is quite acceptable.'

'Really?' said Liza.

'Yes, really,' said the bear.

'Now – what is the word for something you can't stand – ten letters?'

'I don't know,' said Liza.

'Unbearable,' said the bear.

'That's brilliant,' said Liza.

'Yes, I told you I was,' smiled the bear.

He leapt up and started to dance again.

'I dance the tango best of all,' he said.

'What's the tango?' asked Liza.

The bear took a rose from the vase, placed it between his teeth, grabbed Liza round the waist and marched up and down the room, singing and leaping and hurling Liza around with him until she fell down in a breathless heap.

'Now that,' said the bear, 'was the tango. Of course, you have to practise a lot before you can do it as well as me. What's upstairs?' he said, already going up them.

'My room,' said Liza, as the bear flung open the door.

'It needs trees,' said the bear.

'Trees?' said Liza.

'Definitely,' said the bear. 'A few big trees growing in here would give it style, make it more like a forest.'

'But people don't have trees growing inside their rooms,' said Liza. 'And who'd want to live in a forest?'

'Bears,' said the bear, picking up Liza's school coat. He tried to put it on and it split right down the middle.

'Badly made,' said the bear, throwing it in the wastepaper basket.

'You were too big for it,' said Liza, wondering what she'd wear for school on Monday.

'No, no,' said the bear, 'if a coat doesn't fit a bear, there's something wrong with the coat – not something wrong with the bear. Always remember that.'

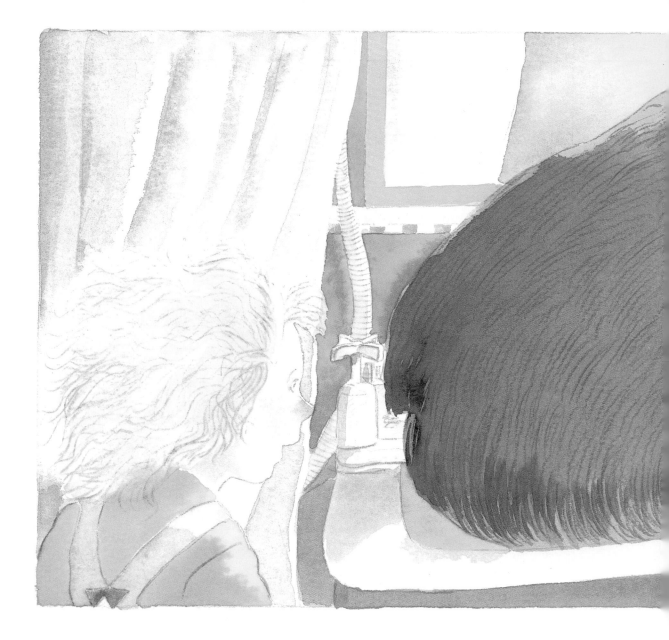

He went into the bathroom and climbed into the bath. It was a very tight fit.

'This bath is too small,' said the bear.

'Well, it's big enough for me,' said Liza.

'What's the use of that if it's not big enough for a bear?' he said.

Liza heard her mother come in; she'd been chatting to the next-door neighbour. 'Time for tea,' she called upstairs.

'There's a bear in our bath,' shouted Liza.

'Is there, darling? That's nice. What's his name?'

'Jam,' shouted Liza.

'Oh, I forgot to get it. Never mind, I'll get some tomorrow.' She started to lay the table. Liza went back to the bathroom.

The bear was drinking hair shampoo and wearing a pair of frilly knickers on his head.
'How do I look?' he said.
'You look like a bear with a pair of frilly knickers on your head,' said Liza, but the bear had already disappeared into Liza's brother's room.

Jack was standing up in his cot, looking rosy from his nap.
'Teddy,' he said, pointing at Jam and dribbling with excitement.
'No, Jam,' said the bear. 'He's not very bright, is he?'
'Well, he's only two,' said Liza.
'When I was two, I could count up to 1,104 and play the violin,' said the bear, scooping Jack out of his cot.

Liza's mother shouted up the stairs. 'Liza, have you finished your homework yet?'

'Mummy,' shouted Liza, 'there's a bear in Jack's room giving Jack a bear hug.'

'That's nice,' said her mother. 'Tell Jack to say thank you.'

'I think it's time to go,' said the bear.

'Where to?' asked Liza.

'Oh, just somewhere,' said the bear, vaguely. 'I lead a very busy life, you know. I've got a singing lesson at four.'

'I didn't know that bears sang,' said Liza.

'Let's face it,' said the bear, 'you didn't know much about bears at all until you met me.'

'That's true,' said Liza.

'What will you do when I've gone?' asked the bear.

'I have to do my homework,' said Liza. 'I have to write about what I've done today.'

'That's easy,' said the bear. 'Just write that you met this totally wonderful, clever, fascinating bear.'

'No one would believe me,' said Liza.

And they didn't!

Spider the
Horrible Cat

Nanette Newman

Once upon a time, not so long ago – well, last winter, in fact – there lived a cat named Spider.

He wasn't the sort of cat you usually read about. He was untidy, wriggly, fat in some places, thin in others, snarly, scratchy, and very, very mean.

He could be nasty about almost anything. For instance, if his breakfast wasn't there at eight on the dot, he would screech wildly and run up and down the stairs twenty times. He would thump his tail against the fridge, claw the best cushion in the big chair, and leap onto the mantelpiece, knocking over the photograph of himself with his owner, a dear, sweet, old lady named Mrs Broom.

84

Now, Mrs Broom, unlike her cat, was kind and gentle and very, very quiet. She was fat in some places and thin in others, but apart from that she was nothing like her cat at all.

You might wonder how such a horrible cat came to live with such a lovely person. In fact, most people wondered just that – most people except Mrs Broom, who wasn't the wondering type.

The truth of the matter was he just arrived.

It was on a day when everyone woke up, looked out of their windows, and said, 'What a beastly, cold, rainy, dreary day,' that Mrs Broom went to her front door to bring in the milk and ... discovered a cat.

'Well, would you believe it,' she said. 'A dear little cat.'

Now, this was a *big* mistake, for he wasn't a dear little cat at all. He sat there in the rain, making faces and crossing his eyes, a habit he had when he was very, very annoyed (which, of course, he always was).

As soon as he saw Mrs Broom, he had one of his tantrums. He lay on his back, waved his paws in the air, and screamed in a very alarming way.

But Mrs Broom didn't seem to notice. She just picked up the bottles and disappeared into the kitchen. After a while, the cat decided to stop showing off and followed her. What he saw would have made most cats happy, but not this cat. Mrs Broom was singing as she chopped up fish and poured some cream into a bowl.

The horrible cat banged his tail on the floor and snarled, showing all his teeth. Mrs Broom turned to look at him, and because she couldn't see very well without her glasses, which she had left by the bed, she said, 'Oh, you dear little thing, you're smiling at me.'

Mrs Broom put down the delicious breakfast. At first the cat pretended he couldn't care less and turned his back on it. Then, when Mrs Broom wasn't looking, he pounced on the food, spilling as much as possible, slopping cream onto the floor, and letting bits of fish fall out of the sides of his mouth. It was a very unattractive sight. Most people would have tried not to look, but Mrs Broom just cleaned up the mess and said, 'Well, you really enjoyed that, didn't you?'

The cat gave her one of his meanest looks.

'I think you'd better stay with me,' Mrs Broom said. And that's how it happened – as simple as that.

After that first morning things went from bad to worse. For instance, the horrible cat had never had a name and Mrs Broom had never had a cat, so she wasn't very good at thinking of catlike names. She had, how-ever, always been rather fond of spiders. 'I'll call you Spider,' she said, as he tried to claw the quilt off her bed. 'You'll like that!' He didn't, of course – because he didn't like anything.

90

Spider's days were always busy. He chased every dog that came near the house. He walked all over Mrs Broom's ironing with muddy paws. He ran up trees and made such a fuss that all the birds left their nests.

One day Mr Knight, who lived nearby, saw Spider hanging from a top branch, and, being a kind man, he got a ladder to help him down. But when Mr Knight reached him, Spider stuck out his tongue and slid down on his own. Next he jumped into Mrs Broom's bath, licked the soap, and covered the towels with hair. He frightened the baby who lived next door by taking her teddy bear and sitting on it. And all that was before lunch!

Every day he tore the newspaper into small pieces and chewed up the bills. When he saw the white cat from across the street he spat three times, stuck out his claws, and made his fur stand up like a brush.

In the evening Mrs Broom liked to watch television. She particularly liked quiz shows, but Spider soon learned to change the channels with his nose. Mrs Broom never seemed to notice.

When Mrs Broom went to bed, Spider would climb on top of the wardrobe and then leap onto her quilt. He'd toss and turn and jump around until finally even he was exhausted. Then he'd poke his head out from under the covers to see if Mrs Broom was annoyed. But she was always fast asleep with a smile on her face.

Mrs Broom's friend Emily came to tea one day. She was horrified when Spider jumped on her head and rearranged her hair in a most unattractive way, then knocked over the milk jug and kicked the biscuits in the air with his back paws. Mrs Broom laughed. 'He's doing all his little tricks for you,' she said.

'Isn't he funny?' Emily didn't think he was at all funny and said to Mr Knight later that she'd seen some horrible animals in her time, but never one as horrible as Spider. Mr Knight, who never had a bad word to say about anyone, had a very bad word to say about Spider – so bad, in fact, that Emily wondered whether she had heard him correctly.

Spider was still living with Mrs Broom when the summer came. Mrs Broom loved being in her garden. She grew lots of flowers, herbs, and lettuces – or she did before she had Spider. He decided the best place for a nap was the lettuce bed, so that was the end of those.

Most afternoons, Spider lay by
the side of the fish pond with
one paw dangling in the water
so that the fish were always in a
panic, fearing for their lives. Mrs
Broom didn't notice. She just
blew him a kiss as she picked
some roses for the house.

It was a day in July, when everyone
looked out of their windows and said, 'Oh,
what a beautiful, hot summer day,' when
something happened that changed Spider's life.

He'd been sitting on the wall trying to outstare
the thrush in the apple tree when he heard a
gentle thud. He looked around and there, lying
half on the herb bed and half on the path, was
Mrs Broom. Spider leapt from the wall straight
onto Mrs Broom's tummy, but she didn't move.
He made some of his scary faces and did a bit
of yowling, but Mrs Broom was very still and
her eyes were tightly shut.

For the first time in Spider's life he was
frightened. He felt very strange as he looked
at Mrs Broom's white face. He tried licking her
cheek, but even though it was a hot day she felt
cold. He thumped his tail and rolled on his back
like he did when he wanted some food, but Mrs
Broom just lay very still.

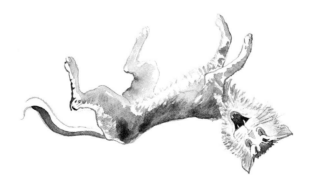

98

Spider knew that something was dreadfully wrong and he must get help. But how? He ran around Mrs Broom's body trying to think, and then he sped off to Emily's house as fast as he could.

Emily was knitting in a deck chair in her garden. Spider jumped onto her lap and started to meow. Emily pushed him off, shouting, 'Get away, you nasty, naughty cat. Get away!'

So Spider ran off to Mr Knight's house. Mr Knight was tying up his string beans. When he saw Spider he picked up his shovel and said, 'Come anywhere near these and you'll know what for.' Desperate, Spider picked up the ball of string in his mouth and started to run, unwinding it as he went. Mr Knight shouted, 'Drop that string! Come back here!' and started to run after him.

Spider ran and ran, out of the garden, across the road,
through Emily's garden, round the big chestnut tree, and into
Mrs Broom's garden. He came to a stop
by Mrs Broom's left foot. He heard
Mr Knight come clumping up the path
with the other end of the string in his
hand, saying, 'I'll get you for this!'

But he stopped when he saw Mrs Broom with Spider waiting beside her. Mr Knight immediately called an ambulance, and soon Mrs Broom was on her way to the hospital.

Suddenly alone, Spider didn't know what to do with himself. The house felt very empty. There was no one to make him nice meals, no one to tell him he was adorable, and no one to annoy. As the days went by he grew so depressed that he didn't even feel like frightening the white cat across the road. One day a big dog came into the garden and started to bark, but Spider did nothing. There were no singing sounds in the house, and the flowers in the vase all dropped their petals. Life just wasn't the same.

At night Spider had to forage around in dustbins for food that had been thrown away, and during the day he didn't feel like rushing around and being nasty and annoying. After all, there was no one to be nasty to. He grew thinner and thinner and sat around in an unhappy heap, thinking about things.

It was a Thursday, when the leaves were beginning to turn brown and when people were opening their windows and saying, 'Well, isn't this a fine autumn morning,' when Spider heard the front door open. He looked up from where he was lying on the kitchen floor and there, to his amazement, was Mrs Broom. She looked much the same as ever, and when she saw Spider she smiled and smiled.

'Oh, my goodness me,' she said. 'Just look at you. I've been so worried about you, I couldn't wait to get back. You look like you could use a good meal.' Before Spider could move she had taken off her coat and was bustling around in the kitchen, fixing him something tasty. The old Spider would have done a bit of snarling and knocked the plate over and spat and thumped his tail, but to tell the truth, he was so thrilled to see Mrs Broom and to have a good meal that he forgot to do any of these things.

That evening, when Mrs Broom had tidied the house and was watching television with her feet up, Spider did something he had never done in his life before. He crawled into her lap, curled up into a ball, and started to purr. 'Well, well,' said Mrs Broom. 'What's all this?' And she stroked the back of his head until they both fell asleep.

Of course, word got around how clever Spider had been when Mrs Broom had her fall, and how he had found a way to get Mr Knight to follow him. In fact, Spider became quite famous. Even Emily was impressed that a cat, particularly a cat as horrible as Spider, could have thought of such a kind and clever thing to do. And as for Mr Knight, he told the story forevermore to anyone who would listen, always ending it with, 'And that cat, Spider, really saved Mrs Broom's life.'

It goes without saying that Mrs Broom and Spider are still living happily together.

Spider doesn't make faces anymore, or have tantrums, or claw people, or whine, or rush around in a frenzy. Some say it's because he's older and wiser, but others say it's because he's found someone to love.

As for Mrs Broom, she loved Spider anyway, even when he was nasty. So she just goes on the way she always did.

There's a Bear
in the Classroom

Nanette Newman

Liza sat alone in the corner of the classroom and tried not to cry. A big tear fell out of her right eye, but before she could brush it away she heard a voice say, 'Not going to cry, are you?'

Liza looked up and saw a very large bear sitting on top of a desk. 'Are you speaking to me?' she asked.

'I expect so,' said the bear, 'as we're the only two here.'

'Oh,' said Liza.

'Well, are you?' said the bear.

Liza could feel the tear running slowly down her nose.

'Am I what?' she said.

'Going to cry?' asked the bear.

'Well, I was thinking about it,' she said, 'but I don't think I will now.'

'Phew! Thank goodness for that,' said the bear, coming over to Liza and picking up her school bag and hanging it around his neck. 'Two things really upset me – grizzling girls and blubbering bears.'

'Oh,' said Liza as the bear started to rummage through h bag. 'I don't grizzle very often, but I was feeling sad beca I don't have a best friend.'

'Well, you do now,' said the bear, as he spilt everything out of Liza's pencil case and wound her school scarf around his head. 'Me!'

'You?' said Liza.

'Being a best friend is one of the things I'm brilliant at.'

'Is it?' said Liza, watching him eat her apple in two bites.

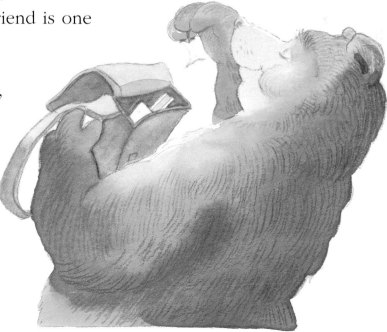

'From now on you can tell everyone you have this wonderful, exciting, clever best friend called Jam.'

'Oh yes,' said Liza, 'I'd forgotten your name was Jam. We've met before.' She tried hard not to giggle because it seemed such a very odd name, even for a bear.

'What's yours?' asked Jam.

'My name is Liza.'

The bear stopped balancing a ruler on his nose and said, 'Liza? Your name is Liza?' He started to laugh. He lay down on the floor and kicked his legs in the air, holding his sides and rocking backwards and forwards as his laugh grew louder and louder. 'What a funny name,' he said.

'I don't think so,' said Liza.

'Oh yes,' said Jam, jumping to his feet. 'What a pity you couldn't have been called something usual, like Jelly.'

Liza watched as he went to a desk belonging to one of her classmates called Archie and tried to sit in his chair. It was a very tight squeeze.

'These desks are too small,' he said. 'A bear could get stuck. You should speak to someone about that.'

'Well, they're really made for children,' said Liza.

'Tut, tut, I don't know what schools are coming to,' said Jam, shaking his head. He lifted the desk lid. 'I feel peckish. Anything delicious to eat in here?'

Liza rushed over to him. 'That's Archie's desk and I don't think he'd like it if we took anything out of it.'

'He'd love it,' said Jam, managing to find a half-eaten chocolate bar. 'People should always have something handy to feed a hungry bear, don't you agree?'

'I suppose so,' said Liza, not sure if Archie would understand.

Jam got up, walked over to the blackboard and rubbed out: 'HOW MANY WIVES DID HENRY VIII HAVE?'

'Our history teacher wrote that,' said Liza, hoping she wouldn't get the blame, but Jam wasn't listening. He had picked up a piece of chalk and had written in big letters: 'HOW MANY BEARS DID HENRY VIII HAVE?'

Then he sat down at the teacher's desk and started looking through a pile of exercise books.

'That's our maths homework,' said Liza.

'Really?' said Jam. 'Maths is one of my favourite subjects.'

'I wish it was mine,' said Liza. 'I'm always bottom of the class.'

Jam was marking the books with a red pencil. He looked up. 'The best way to do maths is standing on your head.'

'Why?' asked Liza.

'Because everything looks clearer from upside down,' explained Jam. He stood on his head to demonstrate. 'Ask me a maths question,' he said.

'Er…' Liza tried to think of one.

'Ask me,' suggested Jam, 'how do you get four bears into a car.'

'All right,' said Liza. 'How do you get four bears in a car?'

'Two in the front and two in the back,' said Jam. 'Correct. See what I mean? Now you try.'

Liza tried, but each time she stood on her head, she wobbled back down again.

'Let me help you,' said Jam. 'After all, what are best friends for?'

Liza kicked up her legs and Jam caught them. 'How does everything look?' he asked.

'Upside down,' said Liza.

'Exactly. Now let me give you a maths test... Four bears are having a picnic, and two friends join them and they eat all the cake and the peanut-butter sandwiches and the chocolate biscuits and the trifle and ice-cream in five minutes. How do they feel?'

'Sick,' said Liza, feeling a bit sick herself from standing on her head.

'Precisely,' said Jam. 'The answer is six. There, you see, it works. You go to the top of the class.'

'Actually, what I said was...' Liza started to say as she stood up straight again, feeling very giddy, but the bear wasn't listening.

'I am a superb teacher,' said Jam. He tore a page out of one of the exercise books and folded it into a paper hat which he placed over one ear. 'Can I see the rest of the school?' he asked.

'Well,' said Liza, 'would you like to see the hall where we do ballet and rehearse for the school play?'

'Acting and dancing,' said the bear, already on his way out of the classroom, 'are two of my favourite things.'

Liza looked up and down the corridor, but there was nobody else about. 'This way,' she said.

Jam was humming a tune and hopping on one leg when Liza heard the Headmistress call out from her office, 'Is that you, Liza?'

Jam stopped hopping and listened.

'Yes, Miss Hopkins,' said Liza. 'I'm just showing my new best friend around the school.'

'That's nice,' said Miss Hopkins. 'Don't forget, your mother will be here to collect you in ten minutes.'

'I won't,' said Liza.

'What's your friend's name?' asked Miss Hopkins.

Liza put her head around the door of her office. 'Jam,' Liza said, 'and he's a bear.'

There was a thud as Miss Hopkins fell to the floor in a faint. 'Funny woman,' said Jam, taking a quick look.

They reached the hall without seeing anyone else, which Liza thought was just as well.

'A piano!' said Jam, rushing over to it and lifting the lid. 'What would you like me to play?'

'*Can* you play?' asked Liza.

'Can I *play*? I give concerts!' replied Jam.

'Do you know the music from the ballet *Swan Lake*?'

'Well, of course,' said Jam, 'but every bear plays that. Let me think of something special.'

Staring at the ceiling, he started to thump the keys. Then he began to sing:

'Mary, Mary, quite contrary,
How do your little bears grow?
With eyes like shells,
And fur that smells,
Oh, pretty bears all in a row.'

When he had finished, he stood up and took a bow. 'You can clap now,' he said.

Liza clapped.

'I wrote that myself,' Jam said.

Liza was too polite to say it sounded very much like a nursery rhyme she had heard before.

'Shall we dance?' asked Jam, going over to a big wicker basket in which all the costumes for the school play were kept. He opened it.

'We've been practising The Dance of the Sugar Plum Fairy,' said Liza.

'Perfect!' said Jam, pulling out all the costumes and hurling them all over the place. 'One of my favourites.'

'I'll just go and get my ballet shoes,' said Liza.

When she came back, Jam was wearing a pink net ballet skirt which had split, because it was much too small to go around his waist, a hat with roses on it, and he had a ballet shoe dangling from one ear.

'I'm just getting warmed up,' he said, bending down and touching his toes so that the ballet skirt split even more.

'Ready now,' he said, taking Liza's hand and leading her to the middle of the hall. 'Ladies and Gentlemen,' he announced, 'we are proud to present, for one performance only, Liza and Jam dancing The Sugar Plum Bears.'

They started to dance and Liza wondered what her ballet teacher would say if she could see them. They twirled and twisted and whirled about. Jam lifted Liza into the air and spun her around in circles until the dance came to an end.

Jam gave a very deep bow and Liza curtseyed.

'Thank you, thank you for your applause,' said Jam, bowing again and again to an imaginary audience.

It was then that Liza heard her mother calling, 'Liza, are you
ready? It's time to go.'

'I'm coming, Mummy,' shouted Liza. 'I just have to say
goodbye to my best friend, Jam.'

She started to put on her shoes and school blazer. 'He's
a bear,' she added.

'Your best friend is bare?' said her mother. 'Well, tell her
to put some clothes on. It's very cold outside.'

'I have to go,' said Liza to Jam.

'So do I,' he replied. 'I have a million things to do and I'm
playing tennis at four.'

'I never had such a clever friend,' said Liza.

'*Best* friend,' said Jam.

'Best friend,' agreed Liza.

She went down the corridor and outside to where her mother was waiting.

'Sorry I was late,' said Liza's mother.

'It didn't matter a bit,' said Liza.

And it didn't.

The Beast with a Thousand Teeth

Terry Jones

 long time ago, in a land far away, the most terrible beast that ever lived roamed the countryside. It had four eyes, six legs and a thousand teeth. In the morning it would gobble up men as they went to work in the fields. In the afternoon it would break into lonely farms and eat up mothers and children as they sat down to lunch, and at night it would stalk the streets of the towns, looking for its supper.

In the biggest of all the towns, there lived a pastry cook and his wife, and they had a small son whose name was Sam. One morning, as Sam was helping his father to make pastries, he heard that the mayor had offered a reward of ten bags of gold to anyone who could rid the city of the beast.

'Oh,' said Sam, 'wouldn't I just like to win those ten bags of gold!'

'Nonsense!' said his father. 'Put those pastries in the oven.'

That afternoon they heard that the king himself had offered a reward of a hundred bags of gold to anyone who could rid the kingdom of the beast.

'Oooh! Wouldn't I just like to win those hundred bags of gold,' said Sam.

'You're too small,' said his father. 'Now run along and take those cakes to the palace before it gets dark.'

So Sam set off for the palace with a tray of cakes balanced on his head. But he was so busy thinking of the hundred bags of gold that he lost his way, and soon it began to grow dark.

'Oh dear!' said Sam. 'The beast will be coming soon to look for his supper. I'd better hurry home.'

So he turned and started to hurry home as fast as he could. But he was utterly and completely lost, and he didn't know which way to turn. Soon it grew very dark. The streets were deserted, and everyone was safe inside, and had bolted and barred their doors for fear of the beast.

Poor Sam ran up this street and down the next, but he couldn't find the way home. Then suddenly – in the distance – he heard a sound like thunder, and he knew that the beast with a thousand teeth was approaching the city!

Sam ran up to the nearest house, and started to bang on the door.

'Let me in!' he cried. 'I'm out in the streets, and the beast is approaching the city! Listen!' And he could hear the sound of the beast getting nearer and nearer. The ground shook and the windows rattled in their frames. But the people inside said no – if they opened the door, the beast might get in and eat them too.

So poor Sam ran up to the next house, and banged as hard as he could on their door, but the people told him to go away.

Then he heard a roar, and he heard the beast coming down the street, and he ran as hard as he could. But no matter how hard he ran, he could hear the beast getting nearer … and nearer… And he glanced over his shoulder – and there it was at the end of the street! Poor Sam in his fright dropped his tray, and hid under some steps. And the beast got nearer and nearer until it was right on top of him, and it bent down and its terrible jaws went SNACK! and it gobbled up the tray of cakes, and then it turned on Sam.

Sam plucked up all his courage and shouted as loud as he could: 'Don't eat me, Beast! Wouldn't you rather have some more cakes?'

The beast stopped and looked at Sam, and then it looked back at the empty tray, and it said:

'Well ... they *were* very nice cakes... I liked the pink ones particularly. But there are no more left, so I'll just have to eat you...' And it reached under the steps where poor Sam was hiding, and pulled him out in its great horny claws.

'Oh ... p-p-please!' cried Sam. 'If you don't eat me, I'll make you some more. I'll make you lots of good things, for I'm the son of the best pastry cook in the land.'

'Will you make more of those pink ones?' asked the beast.

'Oh yes! I'll make as many pink ones as you can eat!' cried Sam.

'Very well,' said the beast, and put poor Sam in its pocket, and carried him home to its lair.

The beast lived in a dark and dismal cave. The floor was littered with the bones of the people it had eaten, and the stone walls were marked with lines, where the beast used to sharpen its teeth. But Sam got to work right away, and started to bake

as many cakes as he could for the beast. And when he ran out
of flour or eggs or anything else, the beast would run back into
town to get them, although it never paid for anything.

Sam cooked and baked, and he made scones and éclairs and
meringues and sponge cakes and shortbread and doughnuts.
But the beast looked at them and said, 'You haven't made any
pink ones!'

'Just a minute!' said Sam, and he took all the cakes and he
covered every one of them in pink icing. 'There you are,' said
Sam, 'they're all pink ones!'

'Great!' said the beast and ate the lot.

153

Well, the beast grew so fond of Sam's cakes that it shortly gave up eating people altogether, and it stayed at home in its cave, eating and eating and growing fatter and fatter. This went on for a whole year, until one morning Sam woke up to find the beast rolling around groaning and beating the floor of the cave. Of course you can guess what was the matter with it.

'Oh dear,' said Sam, 'I'm afraid it's all that pink icing that has given you toothache.'

Well, the toothache got worse and worse and, because the beast had a thousand teeth, it was soon suffering from the worst toothache that anyone in the whole history of the world has ever suffered from. It lay on its side and held its head and roared in agony, until Sam began to feel quite sorry for it. The beast howled and howled with pain, until it could stand it no longer. 'Please, Sam, help me!' it cried.

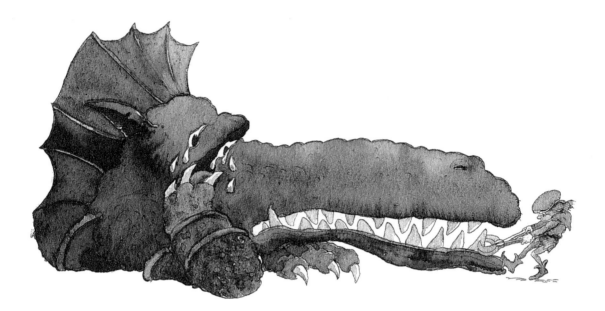

'Very well,' said Sam. 'Sit still and open your mouth.'

So the beast sat very still and opened its mouth while Sam got a pair of pliers and took out every single tooth in that beast's head.

Well, when the beast had lost all its thousand teeth, it couldn't eat people any more. So Sam took it home and went to the mayor and claimed ten bags of gold as his reward.

Then he went to the king and claimed the hundred bags of gold as his reward. Then he went back and lived with his father and mother once more, and the beast helped in the pastry shop, and took cakes to the palace every day, and everyone forgot they had ever been afraid of the beast with a thousand teeth.

The
Fly-by-Night

Terry Jones

A little girl was lying in bed one night when she heard a tapping on her window. She was rather frightened, but she went to the window and opened it, telling herself that it was probably just the wind. But when she looked out, do you know what she saw? It was a little creature as black as soot with bright yellow eyes, and it was sitting on a cat that appeared to be flying.

'Hello,' said the creature, 'would you like to come flying?'

'Yes, *please*!' said the little girl, and she climbed out of the window on to the cat and off they flew.

'Hang on tight!' cried the creature.

'Where are we going?' asked the little girl.

'I don't know!' called the creature.

'Who are you?' asked the little girl.

'I haven't got a name,' said the creature, 'I'm just a fly-by-night!' And up they went into the air, over the hills and away.

The little girl looked around her at the bright moon and the stars that seemed to wink at her and chuckle to themselves. Then she looked down at the black world below her, and she was suddenly frightened again, and said: 'How will we find our way back?'

'Oh! Don't worry about *that*!' cried the fly-by-night. 'What does it matter?' And he leant on the cat's whiskers and down they swooped towards the dark earth.

'But I must be able to get home!' cried the little girl. 'My mother and father will wonder where I am!'

'Oh! Poop-de-doo!' cried the fly-by-night, and he pulled back on the cat's whiskers and up they soared – up and up into the stars again, and all the stars were humming in rhythm:

> Boodle-dum-dee
> Boodle-dum-da,
> Isn't it great,
> Being a star!

And all the stars had hands, and they started clapping together in unison. Then suddenly the moon opened his mouth and sang in a loud booming voice:

> I'm just the moon,
> But that's fine by me
> As long as I hear that
> Boodle-dum-dee!

And the cat opened its mouth wide and sang: 'Wheeeeeeee!' and they looped-the-loop and turned circles to the rhythm of the stars.

But the little girl started to cry and said: 'Oh please, I want to go home!'

'Oh no you don't!' cried the fly-by-night, and took the cat straight up as fast as they could go, and the stars seemed to flash past them like silver darts.

'Please!' cried the little girl. 'Take me back!'

'Spoilsport!' yelled the fly-by-night and he stopped the cat dead, then tipped it over, and down they swooped so fast that they left their stomachs behind them at the top, and landed on a silent hill.

'Here you are!' said the fly-by-night.

'But this isn't my home,' said the little girl, looking around at the dark, lonely countryside.

'Oh! It'll be around somewhere, I expect,' said the fly-by-night.

'But we've come miles and miles from my home!' cried the little girl.

But it was too late. The fly-by-night had pulled back on the cat's whiskers and away he soared up into the night sky, and the last the little girl saw of him was a black shape silhouetted against the moon.

    The little girl shivered and looked around her, wondering if there were any wild animals about.

    'Which way should I go?' she wondered.

    'Try the path through the wood,' said a stone at her feet.

So she set off along the path that led through the dark wood.

As soon as she got amongst the trees, the leaves blotted out the light of the moon, branches clutched at her hair, and roots tried to trip up her feet, and she thought she heard the trees snigger, quietly; and they seemed to say to each other: 'That'll teach her to go off with a fly-by-night!'

Suddenly she felt a cold hand gripping her neck, but it was just a cobweb strung with dew. And she heard the spider busy itself with repairs, muttering: 'Tut-tut-tut-tut. She went off with a fly-by-night! Tut-tut-tut-tut.'

As the little girl peered into the wood, she thought she could see eyes watching her and winking to each other, and little voices you couldn't really hear whispered under the broad leaves: 'What a silly girl – to go off with a fly-by-night! She should have known better! Tut-tut-tut-tut.'

Eventually she felt so miserable and so foolish that she just sat down and cried by a still pond.

'Now then, what's the matter?' said a kindly voice.

The little girl looked up, and then all around her, but she couldn't see anyone.

'Who's that?' she asked.

'Look in the pond,' said the voice, and she looked down and saw the reflection of the moon, smiling up at her out of the pond.

'Don't take on so,' said the moon.

'But I've been so silly,' said the little girl, 'and now I'm quite, quite lost and I don't know how I'll *ever* get home.'

'You'll get home all right,' said the moon's reflection. 'Hop on a lily-pad and follow me.'

So the little girl stepped cautiously on to a lily-pad, and the moon's reflection started to move slowly across the pond and then down a stream, and the little girl paddled the lily-pad after it.

Slowly and silently they slipped through the night forest, and then out into the open fields, where they followed the stream until they came to a hill she recognized, and suddenly there was her own house.

180

She ran as fast as she could and climbed in through the
window of her own room and snuggled into her own dear bed.

And the moon smiled in at her through the window, and she
fell asleep thinking how silly she'd been to go off with the
fly-by-night. But, you know, somewhere, deep down inside her,
she half hoped she'd hear another tap on her window one day
and find another fly-by-night offering her a ride on its flying cat.
But she never did.